No One But You

NO ONE BUT YOU

Douglas Wood

ILLUSTRATED BY P.J. Lynch

WALKER BOOKS
AND SUBSIDIARIES

LONDON · BOSTON · SYDNEY · AUCKLAND

There are so many things in the world,

so many important things
    to be taught,
    to be shown.

But the best things,
    the most important ones of all,
    are the ones no one can teach you
    or show you
    or explain.

No one can discover them
    but you.

No one but you can feel the rain kiss your skin
or the wind ruffle your hair.

And no one but you can walk through a rain puddle
in your bare feet.

No one but you can listen with your ears
to the song of a bird in a treetop
or the wind in the pines
or the scolding of a squirrel as he
shakes his tail and stamps his feet.

No one but you can see the morning sun sparkle
    on the water
    as you dangle your toes
    and watch a fish dart behind a rock
    and see the miraculous marching of a water boatman across
       the surface of a pool.

No one but you can gently hold
        a turtle with your own hands
        and count the plates on her back
        and the stripes on her chin,
        feel the hardness of her shell
        and the soft scratching of her claws,
        and imagine what a turtle's life is like
        as she swims back into the blue-green shadows
            of her world.

Only one person can notice
    the hum of a bumblebee on a lazy afternoon
    as he buzzes past your ear
    on his way to a clover patch,
    and that someone is no one but you.

And who else but you will roll a glistening dewdrop
from a rose petal onto your tongue
or savour a red, ripe strawberry
or a golden drop of honey
and know what it tastes like
just to you?

No one but you can smell the moist earth
 after rain,
  discovering just the way it smells to you,
  or catch the fragrance of a tulip
  or apple blossom
  or even a dandelion.

No one else can blow dandelion seeds into the wind
    with your breath
    or whistle with a blade of grass
    held between your two thumbs
    or sing your very own song
    with your very own voice
    in your very own way.

No one but you can gently hold
   a puppy in your arms,
   feel the softness of its fur
   and the warm tickle of its tongue,
   and make it feel safe and cared for
   because it's with you.

No one but you can smile just your smile
or laugh just your laugh.

No one but you can remember
your own memories ...
all the things you've done,
all the places you've been,
with all your favourite people.
And, of course, no one but you can
make your new memories –
the ones still to come.

No one but you can hear frogs
singing on a spring night
under a blanket of stars
just the way you can.

No one else in the world can look up at the stars,
these stars, now,
with your eyes,
and feel your own special place on this earth.

And no one else can wish upon *that* star,
that very one,
from just where you stand
and wish your very own wish.
No one but you.

And no one – no one in all the wide world but you –
    can feel the feelings in your heart,
    knowing that someone loves you ...

and saying the words only your lips can say:
    "I love you, too."

No one but you.

To Kathy Ann, with love
D. W.

For Nicole, Nicholas and Chitra
P. J. L.

With special thanks to Willow, Yasmin, Jason-Mogga,
Emma, Maya, Ben, Sam, Evie, Rosebelle and Chitra

First published 2011 by Walker Books Ltd
87 Vauxhall Walk, London SE11 5HJ

2 4 6 8 10 9 7 5 3 1

Text © 2011 Douglas Wood
Illustrations © 2011 P.J. Lynch

The right of Douglas Wood and P.J. Lynch to be identified as
author and illustrator respectively of this work has been asserted by them
in accordance with the Copyright, Designs and Patents Act 1988

This book has been typeset in Golden Cockerel ITC

Printed in China

British Library Cataloguing in Publication Data:
a catalogue record for this book is available from the British Library

ISBN 978-1-4063-3353-4

www.walker.co.uk